THE MAGE'S SPELL

AN EROTIC FAIRYTALE

VICTORIA RUSH

VOLUME 5

CLOVER'S FANTASY ADVENTURES -
BOOK 5

COPYRIGHT

The Mage's Spell © 2021 Victoria Rush

Cover Design © 2021 PhotoMaras

All Rights Reserved

All characters in this story are over the age of eighteen.

For the uninhibited...

WANT TO AMP UP YOUR SEX LIFE?

Sign up for my newsletter to receive more free books and other steamy stuff. Discover a hundred different ways to wet your whistle!

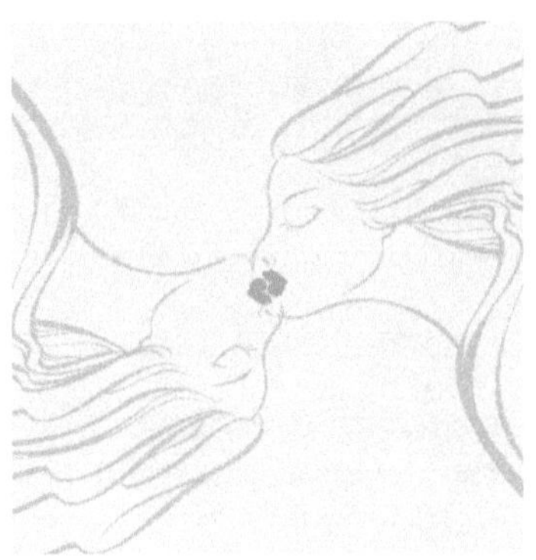

Victoria Rush Erotica

1

———————

After two days of traveling through the forest, Clover and her friends were happy to see a dusty wooden sign announcing their arrival at the outskirts of Longdale. As they walked down the town's main street, they peered up at the storefronts lining the thoroughfare. When Jessop caught sight of a saloon named The Cock and Hen, he grabbed the girls' hands, pulling them in the direction of the swinging doors.

"I don't know about you guys," he said. "But I could use something to eat besides rabbit and grouse. Why don't we stop to rest and recharge our batteries at the local watering hole?"

"Are you sure it's just *food* you're interested in?" Tara said, noticing two scantily dressed women leaning on opposite sides of the doors.

"After our last adventure in the woods," he chuckled, "I think I've had more than enough sex for a few days."

"Speak for yourself," Clover said, winking at one of the girls as they entered the bar.

"Your sexual appetite never ceases to amaze me," Tara

said, shaking her head. "Is *everyone* from your homeland of Tennessee this horny?"

"Probably not," Clover smiled, glancing around the tavern. "I've just got a lot of catching up to do."

Noticing all the tables occupied, the trio ambled up to the counter to order some drinks.

"What'll it be?" a pretty barmaid said, approaching the group.

"Whiskey," Jessop nodded.

"I'll have a beer," Tara said, peering around the room.

"Same," Clover said, glancing down at the barmaid's plump bosom pressed up in her tight decolletage.

Jessop looked upstairs at the overhead balcony, noticing a steady stream of men disappearing into small rooms escorted by half-naked call girls.

"Now I see why they call it the Cock and Hen Saloon," he said, smiling at the barmaid. "What do you have to eat in this place?"

"Our specials today are chicken pot pie and corned beef with cabbage."

"I feel like something warm," he nodded. "I'll have the pie, thank you."

"I could go for something warm too," Clover said, glancing up at the pretty harlots flaunting their wares on the balcony. "Make that two."

"I'll have the corned beef," Tara said, rolling her eyes.

"Two beers and two pot pies, one whiskey, one corned beef," the barmaid nodded. "Be right back."

While she went to pour the drinks, Tara turned around to appraise the room. The noisy lounge was filled with groups of boisterous men playing cards and dart games. But in the back corner of the room sat a lone man with a pointed hat, balancing a levitating ball between his hands.

"Here are your drinks," the barmaid said, placing the glasses in front of the three travelers. "The food will be a couple more minutes."

"What's the story with that odd fellow sitting in the corner?" Tara said, nodding in the direction of the brooding man.

"Oh, you mean *Odarin*?" she said, peering toward his table. "They say he's a mage who can conjure spells. Best you steer clear of him. The last customer who gave him trouble got turned into a goat."

"What *other* powers does he have?" Clover said, her attention temporarily diverted from the preening ladies.

"Invocation, translocation, antimagic," the barmaid said. "The usual hocus-pocus stuff."

"*Translocation?* You mean he has the ability to transport people to different places?"

"So I'm told," the barmaid nodded. "But I couldn't say for sure. Like I said, I try to keep my distance as much as possible."

When the waitress left to retrieve their food orders, Jessop peered at Clover with a wrinkled forehead.

"You weren't actually thinking of *approaching* this character?" he said. "After the crazy warlock and that kinky witch in the woods, haven't you had enough of this magic business?"

"It wouldn't hurt just to talk with him," Clover said, mesmerized by the glowing orb between his hands. "Maybe he can help me get back home."

"Are you still in such a hurry to leave us?" Tara said, placing her hand atop Clover's. "I thought you were starting to enjoy our little adventures together."

"I am," Clover nodded. "I only want to go back for a short while. Just to let my loved ones know I'm okay. Maybe he can help me find the portal to allow me to come and go as I please."

"I suppose it's worth a try," Tara said, squinting at the man suspiciously. "At the very least, we can rest our legs while we see what else he's got up his sleeve."

As the trio wove their way through the cluttered barroom, drunken patrons tried to reach out to pinch and caress the girls' bodies. While Clover and Tara swatted away their hands, Jessop did his best to put himself between his friends and the leering customers. When they finally reached the mage's table, Clover paused, peering at him hopefully.

"Excuse me, sir," she said. "We've been traveling for the last couple of days and just wanted to rest our legs. Do you mind if we join you until we finish our lunch? All the other tables seem to be occupied."

The man darted his eyes between the three friends, then motioned to the empty chairs. Clover noticed the orb that he'd been balancing between his palms still levitated over the table, even when he withdrew his hands.

"Of course," he said. "I can always use the company."

"Thank you," she said, motioning for Jessop to take the seat next to the man while she and Tara sat on the opposite side of the table.

"The barmaid said you have special powers," Clover said, taking a bite of her pie.

"You mean this little *ball trick*?" he said, bouncing the orb softly from side to side with the two sides of one hand.

"She said you also have the ability to transport people from one time and place to another."

"Sometimes," the man nodded. "It depends how far and for how long."

"Have you ever heard of a place called the USA?" Clover said.

The man pinched his eyebrows and shook his head.

"Can't say that I have," he said.

"So you couldn't send me back there?"

"Can you give me a few more details?" the mage said. "In which direction is it?"

"I have no idea," Clover said, shaking her head. "I fell into this land of Abbynthia through a portal in a waterfall a few hundred miles north of here. But it appears to be from a completely different time and place. Maybe a few hundred years in the future..."

"I can only send people to places we both can recognize," the mage said. "I'm sorry, but it looks like I can't help you."

"What *other* powers do you possess?" Tara said, munching on her corned beef sandwich. "The maid said something about invocation and antimagic..."

"Antimagic is the ability to remove spells created by another wizard," he said. "Invocation involves endowing you with special powers."

"We could have used your antimagic powers a few days ago," Jessop chuckled, reflecting back on the witch who'd turned them into half-animal/half-human creatures.

"What *kind* of powers?" Tara said, darting her eyes across the mage's face, trying to assess if he was legit.

"Strength, skill, virility," the mage said. "Everybody seems to want something different."

"Do you charge a fee for these services?" Tara said.

"Not usually," the man said. "It's good practice for me to hone my craft. My powers weaken if I don't use them from time to time."

Tara peered across the table at her friend sitting next to the mage.

"What do you think, Jessop? If you could choose a special power, what would it be?"

"Hmm," he said, peering around the room at the bar patrons still leering at the girls. "All I know is how to fight with a *sword*. If I could be granted one wish, I suppose it would be to be the best swordsman in the land."

"That doesn't sound too difficult," the mage said, passing the orb across the table in Jessop's direction. "Place your hands around the ball, then close your eyes imagining yourself with these powers."

Jessop paused as he peered at the object with its unusual rays surrounding it like an electrified sphere.

"Will it hurt?"

"Not unless you wish for something bad."

Jessop raised his hands and reached out to grasp the sphere, then he closed his eyes for a few moments, trying to concentrate. When he lifted his lids, he turned to face the mage, shaking his head.

"I don't feel anything different," he said.

"You might not be aware of your new powers until they're tested," the mage nodded.

"Tested in what way?"

Suddenly, two drunken bar patrons approached their table, saddling up next to Tara and Clover.

"You girls look like you could use a little different entertainment," one of them said, nodding toward the second-floor balcony. "We've got some *bigger* balls for you to play with if you want to join us upstairs."

Tara turned her head and peered up at the man with a sneer.

"What makes you think I'd be the least bit interested in touching your filthy balls or any *other* part of your stinking body for that matter?" she said.

The man pulled out a knife, placing it next to Tara's pointed ears.

"You better watch how you talk to me and my friend, you little nymph. Otherwise, we might have to teach you some manners–"

Suddenly, Jessop slid out from the other side of the table, pulling his sword from his sheath and snapping the man's knife out of his hand, sending it spinning across the floor.

"What the–" the man said, staggering backwards in surprise.

The second man lunged forward, pulling an equally long sword from his side and brandishing it threateningly toward Jessop.

"Why don't you play with something your *own* size?" he said.

Jessop peered at the man for a moment, then swiped his blade in a criss-cross fashion so quickly the man barely had time to respond, and his pants fell to the floor with his belt cut open at the front. While everyone in the saloon laughed at them, the two men slunk back to the other side of the room, realizing they were badly outmatched.

"Wow," Tara said, smiling at Jessop as he returned to his seat next to the mage. "That was pretty impressive. I've never seen you use your sword so adeptly. Although it really wasn't necessary. I was more than capable of taking care of those two scoundrels my own way."

"I'm sure you were," Jessop said. "But I thought it might be a good opportunity to test my newly acquired powers."

"Were you suitably impressed?"

"Given that I hardly had time to think about it and how I was able to dispatch those two ruffians without anyone even suffering a scratch, I'd have to say yes."

"What about you, Tara?" Clover said, noticing her friend still peering warily at the table of hoodlums. "What would *you* wish for if you could be endowed with special powers?"

"Since my primary weapon of choice is the bow and arrow," she said, "I suppose I'd want to be able to defend myself against any threat, no matter the size or strength of my opponent."

The mage peered across the table at Tara's quiver of handmade arrows slung over her back and nodded.

"Something tells me you're *already* more than capable," he said. "But if you're looking to up your game, grasp the orb and make a wish."

Tara reached out to hold the globe levitating over the table in front of Jessop, then she closed her eyes, clasping onto it tightly. After a few seconds, she released the ball, peering at the mage with a strange smile.

"I feel something different," she said. "Like I'm stronger, faster–and *sharper*."

"You might have a chance to test your new skills sooner than you expected," the mage said, noticing the ruffians approaching their table again with five other hooligans.

"You!" the ringleader shouted, pointing his knife toward Jessop along with each of his friends. "Let's see how fast you are with your sword when you've got a small *army* to contend with."

Jessop began to stand up to confront the mob, but Tara placed her hand gently over his and nodded.

"Let *me* take care of it this time," she said, rising up from her chair and placing an arrow in her bow, pointing it toward the ringleader.

"There's only one of you and *seven* of us," he sneered. "Even if you got lucky enough to spear one of us, we'd be on you before you had time to reload your bow."

Tara hesitated for a moment then she raised her bow a few more inches, firing her arrow through the man's hat, sending it sailing across the room and pinning it against the bullseye of a dartboard on the far side of the saloon wall. The group of hooligans paused for a moment then they all began rushing toward the table. Within the blink of an eye, Tara pulled one arrow after another from her quiver, impaling two of the men in their thigh and one in the foot, stopping them dead in their tracks, squealing in pain. The rest of the group paused for a moment, unsure if they wanted to continue their advance, and when the ringleader took another step forward, she sailed an arrow between his legs, tearing the underside of his pants.

He thrust his hands over his crotch, staring at the elf incredulously.

"You nearly cut off my balls!" he screamed.

"Maybe you should think twice about asking me to *touch* them next time," Tara smiled.

"Come on, boys," the ringleader said, motioning for his friends to exit the saloon. "It looks like this mage is playing his little games again. We'll regroup to fight another day. These two sluts aren't worth the effort anyway."

"Jesus," Clover said when Tara sat back down beside her. "That was *bad-ass!*"

"Not bad if I do say so myself," Tara nodded, smiling toward the mage. "I've never been so fast or accurate with my bow before. You really do have special powers."

"What about you, Clover?" Jessop said, peering across the table at the last member of their triumvirate. "What would *you* wish for if you could have anything you wanted?"

Clover paused for a moment, peering at each of her friends, then she turned toward the magician.

"What if I wanted Jessop's virility and Tara's beauty? Could I have *two* things at once?"

"I suppose you won't know until you try," the mage smiled, nodding toward the floating orb. "Hold the sphere and make your wish. It's worked out pretty well for your friends so far."

Clover looked at her friends, and they nodded softly. Then she reached out to clasp the orb and pinched her eyes closed, imagining her new powers. After a few moments, she felt a strange tingling sensation, then she released the ball with a grunt.

"Well?" Tara said. "Do you feel anything different?"

"It's hard to say," Clover said. "I feel *something* new, that's for sure."

A few seconds later, the pretty barmaid returned to the table to collect their plates.

"I'm sorry for all the trouble," she said. "Some of our customers can get a bit ornery when they get loaded up with too much liquor. The saloon owner watched the whole thing and asked me to apologize. He said the food is on the house. Would you like anything else?"

Clover peered at the barmaid's sexy cleavage, feeling a strange stirring in her loins.

"Can you point me toward the restroom?" she said. "All this excitement seems to have gotten my fluids flowing in the other direction."

"Absolutely," the barmaid said, pointing to the opposite side of the bar. "It's behind the counter, on the left. Let me know if you need anything else."

"Thank you," Clover said, sliding out beside Tara and brushing up against the waitress loading her tray with the empty dishes.

When she entered the lavatory, Clover went into one of

the cubicles and began unbuttoning her snug sheepskin suit, feeling a strange tightening sensation in her crotch. When she pulled down her tunic, she was shocked when a large erect cock sprung up from between her legs.

"What the fuck–?" she said, peering down at the organ incredulously. "What happened to my..."

Reaching down to grasp her new appendage, she moaned, realizing how good it felt to touch it. As she caressed the bulbous head and began to stroke the shaft, she rocked her hips unconsciously, pretending like she was fucking someone.

"Oh my God," she muttered, stoking her dick more rapidly, feeling her pleasure beginning to rise. "Now I know what Jessop means when he says this thing has a mind of its own. This feels incredible."

As she continued to jerk her hard-on with greater excitement, she felt an unusual sensation building up in her balls, and she grasped them tightly, feeling the urge to void. Without warning, she suddenly began spurting long ropes of white cum over the back of the cubicle door while hunched over in delirious pleasure.

"Holy fuck!" she panted. "This thing is amazing! If it feels this good with my *hand*, I can only imagine how good it would feel inside a warm, wet pussy."

While she cleaned up the mess she'd made in the lavatory, she noticed her erection still bobbing excitedly against the front of her abdomen, dripping cum from the top of its throbbing purple head.

"What the hell am I supposed to do with it *now*?" she said, looking at the scrawled pictures of spewing cocks lining the cubicle wall with the names of the bar patron's favorite hookers. "It doesn't seem to want to go down."

Unsure where to stuff her engorged tool, she pulled her

suit back up over her body, angling her boner to one side, trying to make it less noticeable.

"Maybe Jessop can give me some tips on how to quiet this monster," she said to herself. "I can't stay in here all day waiting for it to relax."

As Clover exited the restroom, she bumped into the pretty barmaid returning to the kitchen with another empty food tray.

"Everything okay?" she said, noticing Clover's flushed face and sweaty brow.

"Um, yes," Clover stammered, trying to hide her throbbing erection bulging under her tight sheepskin bodysuit. "I guess I'm still a little worked up after all that excitement at our table."

The barmaid peered down toward Clover's crotch, noticing the long pole swelling in her garment and the wet spot near the tip.

"I see the mage has been busy casting his special *spells* again," she smiled. "It looks like you could use a little help putting that thing to good use. I'm just about to finish my shift. Would you like to go upstairs where I can give you some proper attention?"

Clover peered down at the barmaid's heaving breasts, then glanced up at her with a slack mouth, unsure how to respond. Suddenly, the maid pressed Clover up against the corridor wall, kissing her passionately while grinding her pelvis against Clover's throbbing prick.

"It's okay, sweetheart," the girl said. "I know my way around a dick or two. I'm pretty sure I can get you quieted down before anyone else notices your predicament."

2

———————

When the barmaid returned from the kitchen, she grabbed Clover's hand, leading her upstairs. Before they disappeared into one of the rooms, Clover caught her friends' attention at the table below, giving them a wink to signal where she was going. Tara blew her a kiss and Jessop rolled his tongue over his lips, knowing what she had planned.

You have no idea, Clover thought as the girl closed the door behind her.

"Let's see what we have to work with here, shall we?" the barmaid said, beginning to unbutton Clover's bodysuit.

"Do you bring customers up here often?" Clover smiled, peering down at her pushed-up breasts.

"Only when the mood strikes," the girl said. "And I've been feeling the mood ever since you walked into the bar."

"I'm Clover," Clover said as she began untying the laces holding the top of the girl's frilly blouse together.

"Rae," the bargirl said, pulling Clover's suit down over her breasts. "I see the magician still left you with a *few* girl parts. You're very beautiful."

"Thank you," Clover shuddered, placing her hands around the girl's compressed breasts in her tight-fitting corset and tilting her head down to kiss the tops of them gently. "So are you."

"I've never fucked someone with *tits* before," the barmaid said, grasping Clover's exposed orbs and sucking her nipples.

"You've never been with a woman this way before?"

"Not one equipped with *dick*," the girl said, squeezing Clover's cock under her sheepskin suit still draped over her hips.

"Ungh," Clover groaned, pressing her hips harder against the girl's body, trying to increase the friction.

"The mage endowed you with a pretty good-sized *package*," Rae nodded, pulling Clover's suit down to her ankles, eyeing her bouncing dick inches away from her face. Without warning, she engulfed Clover's cock into her mouth, sliding it all the way down her throat while squeezing Clover's balls with her right hand.

"Holy *fuckkk*," Clover moaned, hunched over in delirious pleasure. "This is *way* better than having a pussy. Suck my cock all the way down to my balls. That feels incredible."

While Clover watched Rae bobbing up and down over her turgid pole, she wondered if the bargirl had honed her skills as a regular working girl. But it hardly mattered at that moment, feeling the familiar tightening sensation in her balls with another orgasm building up inside her like a steam kettle about to explode.

"Oh God, Rae," she grunted. "I'm going to come soon. If you don't want me spewing in your mouth, you better pull back–"

Instead, the bargirl reached behind Clover's ass, gripping her buttocks tightly with both hands while pulling her harder against her face, moaning for Clover to release her pent-up pleasure. Quickly passing the point of no return, Clover placed her hands atop Rae's head and pulled her tight against her crotch while she depositing her load down the girl's throat, grunting in blissful ecstasy. After what seemed like a hundred hard contractions emptying a pint of cum in her mouth, Rae lifted her face off Clover's throbbing dick, peering up at her while licking her lips sensuously.

"*Damn*, girl," she said, standing up to kiss Clover on her mouth. "That magician didn't just give you a bigger *dick* than most men, he also gave you the power to come harder and longer. Maybe I should spend more time getting to know him after all."

"Yeah," Clover panted. "That was the hardest I've come since, well, *ever*."

Rae drifted her hand lower, squeezing Clover's still hard cock firmly in her hand.

"Do you think you'll want to *keep* this thing for a while then?" she said. "Because I know a few other girls and maybe even a couple of men who might *also* want a piece of it."

"I dunno," Clover said, kissing Rae hard as she continued playing with her dripping tool. "I'm still getting used to what it can do. I'm intrigued to see how many times I can get off before it decides it's had enough."

"Well, it's certainly not showing any signs of getting bored yet," Rae smiled, pulling Clover towards the single bed in the room by the end of her dick. "Come on, let's give this thing a right *proper* fucking."

When they reached the footboard, Rae pushed Clover down onto the mattress, then she straddled her stomach while she unbuttoned her corset and pulled off her silk shorts.

"Mmm," Clover hummed, seeing the barmaid's plump

breasts unencumbered for the first time. "You hardly need that corset to hold those pretty tits. Those are the firmest tits I've seen in a long time."

"Not as firm as this *dick* between your legs," Rae said, holding Clover's tool in her hand while she rolled her hips over Clover's stomach. "I've never been with a man who could stay so hard after he came."

"Maybe that's because I'm not a *man*," Clover smiled, pulling Rae on top of her while she thrust her tongue down her throat. "Fuck me with that wet pussy. I want to feel what it's like to make love to another woman with a *real* dick for a change."

"That makes two of us," Rae grunted, sliding her body toward Clover's hips until she felt her dick slapping against her ass.

As she rocked her hips forward and back, Clover's pole bounced between her cheeks like a giant metronome while she rubbed her breasts over Clover's, peering at her with a sly grin.

"God damn, Clover," she panted. "That thing's as hard as an oak tree. I have *got* to try this out for myself sometime."

"I'm sure you'll have plenty of opportunities to suck up to that magician another time," Clover grinned. "Or were you going to just *dream* about having a cock of your own instead of fucking me while you have the chance?"

"Oh, I'm going to *fuck* you alright," the Rae said, raising her hips over Clover's flapping pole and pointing it toward her hole. As she lowered her cunt over Clover's burning tool, both women groaned when they joined lips, kissing each other passionately.

"Holy shit!" Clover moaned, feeling her cock sliding into Rae's juicy tunnel. "So *that's* what it feels like for the man when he sinks his dick into a warm pussy. No wonder they're always checking out every girl's ass everywhere they go. I could get used to this."

"So could *I*," Rae smiled, bouncing her hips over Clover's hard organ while twisting her nipples between her fingers. "I kind of like being able to play with both parts at the same time. You could make a killing in this place if you decided to stay a little longer."

"No thanks," Clover said, reaching up to hold Rae's tits while they shook overtop of her as she humped her dick. "I've already seen how some of your customers treat a lady. I think I'll stick to fucking *women* for the time being."

"That can be arranged too–" Rae grunted.

"There's only *one* woman I want right now," Clover said, grabbing the sides of the Rae's hips and pulling her harder onto her throbbing cock. "I'm going to come so hard inside you, you better hold on to something lest I blow you clear up to the ceiling."

"Yes, baby," Rae purred, squeezing Clover's tits more tightly. "Blow your load deep inside me. I'm going to come with you. You even *fuck* better than a normal man."

"I told you," Clover groaned, digging her nails into the sides of Rae's ass, feeling her cum welling up in her balls. "That's because I'm not a man. I'm a *woman* who just happens to know how to use this thing properly. Are you sure you're ready? I don't know how much longer I can last..."

"Let it rip, hun," Rae smiled, not accustomed to a man waiting for her. "Here it comes..."

Suddenly, Rae threw her head back as her breasts began to tremble on her chest while she pressed her pussy down hard over Clover's rising balls. When she felt Rae spurting her juices over her testicles, Clover leaned forward, holding the bargirl in a tight embrace while spurting her come deep inside Rae's convulsing tunnel. As they both panted and moaned into each other's mouths, they held onto each other for the longest orgasm either one of them had ever experienced.

Holy fuck, Clover murmured to herself, feeling her dick still twitching inside Rae's tight pussy. *I have got to tell Tara about this. Once she knows how much fun it can be to have one of these things, she might want to change her mind about the special powers she chose.*

Jessop too, for that matter, she smiled. *Maybe he can ask the mage to give him two of these. Lord knows there are enough women around here for him to make use of them...*

3

When Clover came downstairs and sat back down at the table, her friends and the mage peered at her and smiled.

"What was *that* all about?" Tara said.

"Let's just say I have a new appreciation why Jessop's world always seems to revolve around his dick."

"Really?" Tara said, reaching under the table to squeeze Clover's still tumescent package. "So *that's* what you wished for."

"Um–hm," Clover nodded. "And it's an amazing thing. Feels completely different than having a pussy."

"I bet," Tara smiled, feeling the wet spot under her sheepskin suit near the end of Clover's throbbing tool. "You're not missing your girly parts then?"

"Thankfully, everything *else* about me seems unchanged. I wasn't quite ready to take on the whole greedy, selfish, egotistical package."

"Hey!" Jessop said, leaning over the table. "Not all men are like that. Just because you have a dick, it doesn't automatically make you an asshole!"

"No, but I now understand why you need to conquer every pussy that crosses your path," Clover smiled. "Your dick does all your thinking for you."

"Sounds about right," Tara nodded, noticing the pretty barmaid approaching their table once again.

"Can I get you anything else?" Rae said, glancing at Clover with a knowing smile.

"I'm feeling pretty satisfied," Clover said, turning to her friends. "How about you guys?"

"Actually," Tara said, feeling Clover's dick growing harder in her hand. "I seem to have worked up a new appetite. How much do you charge for the use of one of your rooms?"

"Just the room?" Rae said.

"I was planning on bringing one of my *own* consorts," Tara smiled as she squeezed Clover's erection.

"I'm sure my manager won't mind if you want to make use of one of the unoccupied rooms for an hour or so. I can run interference for a little while."

"What do you say, Clover?" Tara said, smiling at her friend. "Have you still got a little fuel left in your tank?"

"This motor never seems to want to stop running," Clover said, feeling her cock throbbing at the thought of another wet pussy.

"Good," Tara said, grabbing Clover's hand and pulling her up from the table. "Because my bow isn't the *only* thing feeling charged up right now."

"What about *me*?" Jessop said with a sullen look on his face.

"I didn't know you leaned that way," Tara said with a coy smile.

"She still has all her *other* girl parts," he said, peering at Clover's breasts spilling over the top of her tight bodysuit.

"Plus, you'll be up there with us. You always said you wanted to try it with two men..."

"What do you think, Clover?" Tara said, turning toward her friend. "Do you mind an extra dick competing for your attention?"

"I'm sure we can find some use for it somewhere," Clover smiled. "The more holes, the merrier."

"Can you hold the tab?" Tara said, turning toward the pretty bargirl as the trio headed in the direction of the upstairs lounge. "We shouldn't be too long."

"Take your time," Rae smiled. "I have a feeling your hands are going to be pretty full for the next little while."

As the three friends headed upstairs and across the catwalk, Clover peered down at her table, noticing Rae still talking with the mage.

I have a feeling Tara's fantasy is about to become a little more crowded, she smiled to herself.

When they entered one of the empty rooms and closed the door behind them, Tara didn't waste any time tearing off Clover's clothes and admiring her new accessory with wide eyes.

"Holy shit, Clover," she said. "You weren't kidding when you asked the mage for Jessop's virility. I think your dick is even bigger than *his*!"

"I'm not so sure about that," Jessop said, eyeing Clover's erect tool with more than a passing interest.

"Put your money where your mouth is," Tara smiled. "*Man up*, as you men like to say."

Jessop unbuttoned his belt and when he dropped his pants, his erection bounced up onto his belly in excitement.

"You seem just as turned on by Clover's pretty dick as me," Tara grinned. "Let's see what you guys have to work with."

Tara grasped onto the ends of both their cocks, pulling them closer together. When their dicks touched, she curled her hands around both of their shafts, holding them tightly together.

"It's pretty close," she smiled, noticing pre-cum dribbling out of both peckers. "I'm not sure there's a clear winner in this case, unless you count *me*."

She lowered her head to the top of both cocks and began swirling her tongue around the heads of their joined organs.

"Mmm," she hummed while Clover and Jessop groaned from her ministrations. "So much cock, so little time."

"What exactly did you want to do with us?" Jessop said. "Now that you've fulfilled your fantasy of having two dicks to play with at the same time?"

Tara pulled her mouth away from their throbbing tools for a moment to appraise their impressive girth and length.

"You know what?" she smiled. "You said you wanted to be the greatest swordsman in the land. Let's see how adroitly you can wield that *other* sword of yours."

"You mean like a *dick* fight or something?" Jessop said.

"Exactly," Tara grinned. "Why don't you two put on a little cockfight for me while I lay back and decide who'll be the winner."

Clover and Jessop peered at one another for a moment then Clover stepped forward, slapping the side of her tool firmly against Jessop's. Before long, the two friends were jousting their dicks together playfully as their precum began oozing over the top of their purple heads. After a few moments, Jessop leaned forward to pinch Clover's nipples and within seconds they merged together, rubbing their dicks against one another's bellies while they kissed passionately.

"Hey!" Tara said, wedging herself between the two of them. "This was supposed to be *my* fantasy, not yours! Now get down on the bed, both of you, while I decide which of your pretty peckers I want to take first."

Jessop paused for a moment, noticing the narrow bed was barely wide enough for one person, let alone three.

"How do you want us to position ourselves exactly?"

Tara peered at the skinny bed frame, then a wide grin began to spread across her face.

"Lie down facing one another with your feet beside each other's head. If you guys are so interested in rubbing your dicks together, I've got an idea how we might be able to make it a little more interesting."

Clover and Jessop lay down on the bed on opposite ends, and as they scrunched their hips together and touched balls, their cocks bounced excitedly over their hips, dripping streams of cum down the sides of their long shafts.

"Now *that's* what I call a dream fountain," Tara smiled, tearing off her clothes and straddling Clover's stomach, facing toward her. "I think I'd like to make another wish while I have a chance..."

She raised herself up on her knees then reached between her legs to grasp the ends of their two cocks, pointing them toward her dripping hole.

"We've always thought of ourselves as the Three Musketeers," she smiled. "Now we finally have a chance to be truly united. One for all and all for one–"

As she slowly pressed her tight pussy overtop of their connected cocks, Clover and Jessop groaned in delirious pleasure.

"Oh my God, Tara," Clover shuddered. "I had no idea you could fit both of us inside you. This feels incredible..."

"Better than fucking the pretty barmaid solo?"

"Fuck, yes," Clover panted. "Feeling Jessop's dick against mine makes it twice as good."

"What about you, Jessop?" Tara said, turning her head around to see Jessop tilting his head upward to take it all in. "Are you enjoying this as much as the rest of us?"

"You have no idea," he grunted. "If you could only see what I'm seeing right now..."

"Do you like feeling Clover's dick rubbing against yours while you fuck me?"

"Like you wouldn't believe," he panted, grasping the sides of Tara's ass while he fucked her hard from behind.

"You don't feel jealous having another dick in the equation? I thought you said there was only room for *one* man in our trio?"

"I wouldn't say she's exactly a man," Jessop grunted, feeling his balls beginning to tighten while he watched Tara's ass bobbing up and down over their joined erections. "The mage said these powers wouldn't last forever. I just want to enjoy her extra endowments while we have the chance."

"Are you thinking the same thing, Clover?" Tara said, twisting Clover's nipples while she flexed her pussy tighter around their cocks. "Are you happy for this to be just a *temporary* arrangement?"

"I like being a girl," Clover smiled, reaching up to squeeze Tara's breasts. "But there's something about having a penis that makes me feel more–"

"Virile?" Tara said, bending down to kiss her on the mouth.

"Something like that," Clover murmured, running her fingers through Tara's hair and caressing her pointed ears.

"You're not the only *ones* finding this twice as stimulating," Tara groaned, beginning to hump their cocks more vigorously. "If having two cocks is twice as good as one, then I'm about to *come* twice as hard too. Do you guys think you can time it so you come with me? Because that would be pretty amazing if we could all come together..."

Suddenly Jessop raised himself up and pulled back his knees, humping Tara's ass from the doggy position.

"I'm ready to explode whenever you guys are," he grunted, slapping his balls against Clover's while pounding Tara's ass.

"Yes, Jessop," Clover panted, feeling the familiar sensation in her balls signaling she was about to come. "I'm going to cum so hard inside Tara's pussy. Don't stop, your dick feels so good sliding against mine."

"I want to feel you both coming inside me so bad," Tara grunted. "I've never felt so close to both of you as I do right now–"

"All for one..." Jessop groaned.

"One for all," Clover hissed.

Suddenly, all three friends screamed at the top of their lungs while erupting in a fountain of combined juices, spraying inside, outside, and all around Tara's tight opening as they shook their bodies together in one writhing, twisted mass. After what seemed like sixty seconds of convulsing overtop one another, Jessop finally collapsed on top of Tara's back while they held each other closely.

Just then, the door creaked open a few inches, and Rae stuck her head through the crack.

"Have you guys got room for one more?" she said. "I gave

the magician an extra order on the house, and he gave me a slightly different kind of tip..."

"I'm not sure there's room in this *particular* spot at the moment," Tara smiled, feeling Clover's and Jessop's cum dripping out of her stretched slit. "But I'm pretty sure we can find a few other ways to keep you amused."

The Three Musketeers indeed, Clover smiled, reflecting back on another one of her favorite fairy tales from back home. *This fantasy adventure just keeps getting better all the time...*

4

———

After everybody finished their business upstairs, they returned to the mage's table to settle their account.

"Have you all been enjoying your new powers?" he smiled, noticing the barmaid adjusting her crotch as she headed back into the kitchen.

"Oh my God, yes," Clover sighed, winking at Jessop. "But how long will this last? As much as I like having a man's penis, I'm going to want my girl parts back eventually."

"Your powers will last as long as you need them, or until you grow tired of them," the mage nodded.

"Are you sure we can't *pay* you for your services?" Tara said, peering around the room for any more signs of trouble. "I have a feeling these powers are going to be of value to us in more ways than one."

"I'm just happy to have the chance to practice my craft with some deserving subjects," he smiled, noticing Rae returning to their table. "I'm pretty sure our barmaid will look after any other needs I might have moving forward."

"Can I get you anything else?" she said, glancing around the table.

"I think you've given us more than enough," Tara smiled, sliding two gold coins across the table toward her.

"Will you be staying any little longer?" Rae asked, slipping the coins into her pocket.

"I think it's time we headed on our way," Tara nodded, noticing the pack of hooligans returning with a larger posse. "Is there a back way out of here? We don't want to cause any more trouble..."

"Meet me by the restrooms in a couple of minutes," Rae nodded, glancing at the group. "I'll see if I can sneak you out the back without anyone noticing."

As she returned to the kitchen, the three friends stood up one by one and walked casually toward the rear of the restaurant. When they all convened next to the ladies' restroom, Rae emerged from the kitchen and unlocked the service entrance door.

"I'm sorry to see you leave so soon," she smiled, giving Clover a peck on the cheek. "I was just starting to enjoy my new toy."

"I suspect there's more than enough girls around here to keep you entertained for a while," Tara said, caressing Rae's dripping dick as she exited the rear door.

"Just be careful where you *put* that thing," Jessop smiled. "It can be a two-edged sword if you're not careful."

"**W**here to now?" Clover said as Rae closed the door behind them.

"So far we've been pretty fortunate heading south," Tara said, peering toward the far end of the main street. "I think

it's best we clear out of these parts before we raise the ire of any more locals."

"You won't get any complaints from me," Clover said, noticing some drunken patrons stumbling out of the alleyway between the two buildings. "Let's take the back route, at least until we're out of town. I've had enough excitement for one day."

As they headed in the opposite direction of the main thoroughfare, after a short while they came across some rolling farmland. One of the farms had a row of apple trees with a cluster of ripe fruit hanging from their branches, and they paused, staring at the succulent treat.

"Are you thinking what I'm thinking?" Jessop said.

"It wouldn't hurt to stock up on supplies," Tara nodded. "We don't know how long it might be until we find the next town."

"I can't see anyone around," Clover said, swiveling her head in both directions. "It doesn't feel right stealing a bunch of apples without asking somebody..."

Tara squinted her eyes, peering toward an open barn door in the distance.

"I see someone working in the barn," she nodded. "Let's go have a look."

As they approached the barn, they saw a pretty farmgirl sitting on a wooden crate, hunched under a cow moving her hands up and down. She was wearing tight denim shorts and a loose cotton shirt tied halfway up her stomach, revealing her ample-sized breasts swinging loosely as she milked the heifer.

"Excuse me," Clover said, knocking softly on the barn door. "We were just wondering if you had any apples for sale?"

The farmgirl looked up at them startled, and Clover

gasped when she saw how beautiful she was. With curly reddish-blonde hair spilling over her open blouse and big bright eyes with long eyelashes, she looked like a sexy version of Pippi Longstocking.

"Um, yes," the girl stammered, rising up from her stool as she wiped her wet hands on the side of her shorts. "My parents are in town picking up supplies, but I'm sure they wouldn't mind if you help yourselves to a few."

Tara glanced at a burlap sack resting on the dusty floor a few inches from the cow's feet.

"Do you mind if we borrow your knapsack to stock up? We're traveling kind of light these days."

"No worries," the girl said, stooping down to pick up the sack as all three friends stared at her tight, heart-shaped ass. "Just bring it back when you've filled up and I'll weigh it to see how much you owe."

"Okay," Tara said, taking the sack from the girl and motioning for her friends to join her in the field.

Clover paused for a moment, peering back in the direction of the cow.

"Do you have some *milk* we can take with us too?" she said, finding it difficult to take her eyes off the girl.

"Yes," the girl said. "I was just starting to fill up the canisters when you arrived. If you give me a few minutes, I can give you as much as you'd like."

"Why don't you guys go ahead and pick the apples?" Clover said, smiling toward her friends. "While I stay and collect the milk."

"*Right,*" Tara said, winking at Clover. "We could use a little extra milk too. We'll be back in a half hour or so."

"Take your time," Clover said, peering at the stack of empty milk containers. "It looks like there's quite a few canisters to fill."

After Tara and Jessop headed out into the field to collect the apples, Clover peered at the pretty farmgirl, glancing toward the cow's nipples poking out under its udder like a bunch of puffy penises.

"Do you want some help with that?" she said, stealing a glance at the cleavage exposed at the top of the girl's open blouse.

"Have you ever milked a cow before?" the girl said, wrinkling her forehead at the strange bulge in Clover's crotch.

"No," Clover smiled. "But I've had plenty of practice pulling *other* fleshy parts. I can't imagine it would be too difficult persuading her to give up her milk."

"You might be surprised," the girl said, pulling the crate out for Clover and placing an empty pail under the cow's belly. "It can be quite a workout for the forearms if you're not used to it."

"Yeah," Clover said, sitting down on the box and extending her hands to grasp the cow's teats. "I've just been starting to get used to it."

"The trick is to squeeze the teats hard while you pull down on them," the girl nodded, watching Clover awkwardly grasping the glands.

"Mmm," Clover said, adjusting her hardening cock under her suit as she watched the squirts of white liquid pouring into the pail. "This is starting to feel familiar..."

As the girl knelt down beside Clover to monitor her technique, her eyes widened when she noticed Clover's lengthening rod under her garment.

"Where do you come from?" the girl said with her chest rise in excitement. "You don't look like you're from around these parts–"

"I'm from a place far, far away," Clover said. "Where we have machines that do this milking for us."

"What kind of machines?" the girl asked.

"Big stainless-steel ones run by elec–"

Clover stopped herself, realizing how ridiculous she sounded talking about technology these people had never even heard of.

"Does *everyone* there look like you?" the girl said, staring at Clover's bulging tool poking up toward her stomach.

"Oh, you mean *this*?" Clover said, caressing the outline of her dick softly with her right hand. "No, this is just a minor adjustment created by a magician I met along the way."

"I've never touched a real cock before," the girl said with wide eyes. "My father never even lets me get close enough to boys to *kiss* them..."

"It's your lucky day then," Clover smiled, standing up to face the girl. "Because I'm not really a boy, I've just been temporarily given the equipment of one."

"What does it feel like?" the girl asked.

"Why don't you see for yourself?" Clover smiled, reaching out to grasp her hand and pull it atop her swelling organ. "It's not so different from these cow teats you've been massaging all these years."

"Wow," the girl said, peering up into Clover's eyes with her soft eyelashes. "It's so warm."

"You have no idea," Clover said. "Do you want to feel it in the *flesh*?"

"Could I?" the girl said. "I've heard so many rumors about these. I've always wondered what they looked like up close..."

Clover began to unbutton her suit, leaning in to kiss the girl softly on her lips.

"I've never been kissed by a *girl* either," she said.

"Well then today is *really* your lucky day," Clover smiled. "Because today, you get *two* for the price of one."

When Clover pulled her suit down over her hips, her hard-on bounced up onto her stomach, and the girl gasped.

"It's much bigger than I imagined..." she said.

"Not so big it will hurt you though," Clover said, pulling the girl's hand overtop of her exposed dick as she moaned softly.

"Huh!" the girl jerked, feeling its slippery head. "It's dripping!"

"That's what it does when it gets excited," Clover smiled. "If you stimulate it enough, it will spurt milk just like a cow."

"How do I properly stimulate it?" the girl said, squeezing Clover's tool with her powerful forearms. "Can you teach me?"

"Not quite *that* firmly," Clover chuckled, bending the girl's fingers back, encouraging her to stroke it more softly. "Imagine you're polishing a brass railing instead of stroking a cow's udder. It feels even better when you massage the sensitive tip."

"Like this?" the girl said, grasping the end of Clover's slippery prick and twisting her fist gently over the end.

"Yes," Clover panted into the girl's ear. "Just like that."

"Can I drink the fluid that comes out the end like a cow's milk?" the girl said, raising her fingers to her lips.

"I suppose so," Clover smiled. "But it's not to everyone's taste. It takes some getting used to..."

"I *like* the taste," the girl said, licking her lips. "It's a bit salty, like the butter we sometimes make on the farm."

"If you keep doing that," Clover panted, feeling her balls beginning to tighten again around the base of her cock. "You're going to create *another* batch of cream pretty soon."

"I've heard about women who sometimes suck a man's penis," the girl said. "Do you mind if I see what that feels like too?"

"Oh God," Clover groaned, dying to feel the girl's lips around her pole. "What if your father comes back..."

"He shouldn't be back for another hour. I want to learn *everything* about how to please a man while I have the chance."

"Okay," Clover said, glancing around the shed to make sure no one else was watching. "But I have to warn you. It won't take long for me to release my milk once you get started. It can be a bit of a shock..."

As the girl lowered herself slowly onto her knees, she stared at the tip of Clover's glistening rod, wrapping both hands around it.

"This is way bigger than a cow's teat," she said

"And a lot more sensitive..." Clover panted as the girl lowered her mouth over the tip.

"Mmm," she hummed, sucking on Clover's tool like a lollypop.

"That feels so good," Clover said, rocking her hips forward and back. "Caress my balls with your hands while you suck the tip. They're sensitive too..."

As the girl began to stroke Clover's tightening balls, Clover peered down, grasping the sides of her face gently.

"Yes, baby," she grunted. "Just like that. Suck on the end of my dick harder. I'm going to come soon."

"Mmm," the girl nodded, eager to see what it felt like to feel a man come for the first time.

As she began to swirl her tongue over Clover's glans, Clover gripped the girl's hair with her fists, feeling the pressure inside her about to explode. But just as she was about to dump her load down the girl's throat, she suddenly heard a loud bellow coming from the side of the barn door.

"What the fuck is this?" an angry middle-aged man

holding a pitchfork yelled, staring at the young girl prostrated over Clover's thick dick. "Who the hell are you?"

Clover pulled back from the girl to face the man and as he darted his eyes over her naked ladyboy figure, he shook his head trying to fathom what he saw.

"Step away from that creature, Ella," he said, peering at the farmgirl. "I don't know what this thing is, but I'm pretty sure a few of my friends will be interested. Lock the barn door then tell your mother to round up the townspeople. I think we're going to have a good old-fashioned *witchburning.*"

5

"*A what?*" Clover said, crossing her hands between her legs, trying to conceal her still-flapping erection.

"You must be a witch to look like *that*," the man said. "I've never seen anyone with both men and women parts. This has to be some kind of sorcery–"

"Yes," Clover said, stepping back as the man drew closer with his pitchfork. "It's magic, but I'm not a witch. I met a man in a bar who turned me into this. It's only temporary..."

"You're damn *right* it's only temporary," the man growled. "I'll soon be putting an end to this obscenity before you have a chance to soil any more innocent farmgirls."

"You're going to burn me *alive*?" Clover said, staring at the man incredulously.

"It's the only way to purge the evil spirits," he nodded. "And to send a message to any other witches who might pass this way. Your kind are not welcome in these parts."

"But I didn't do anything wrong!" Clover protested. "Your daughter wanted–"

"She's far too young to know what she wants," the farmer scowled. "I'll decide when she's ready to consort with a man–a *real* man."

Suddenly the opposite barn door slid open, and a group of rough-looking characters she recognized from the bar entered the stable brandishing knives and heavy stones.

"What have we got here?" the ringleader said, peering down at Clover's flagging tool.

"I'd say it's a *witch*, wouldn't you?" the farmer said, nodding toward his friend. "How else do you explain this abomination?"

"Tell him it's not true!" Clover yelled, pleading with the man. "You know about the mage at the bar. Tell him *he* did this to me!"

"I don't know what you're talking about," the man sneered, grinning at his posse.

It was obvious he was still angry about the drubbing he and his friends had received at the saloon and he was looking for vengeance.

"What are you planning to do with her?" the ringleader said, turning toward the farmer.

"I think there's only one thing we *can* do," the farmer smiled. "We have to teach this witch a lesson. That she can't just come traipsing through our village taking any innocent girl she fancies. Prepare the pyre..."

"The *what?*" Clover wailed. "No! I didn't–"

"Put a rag over her mouth too," the farmer said. "I'm tired of listening to her whining and complaining."

"My pleasure," the ringleader said, picking up a dusty rag and tying it tightly over Clover's lips.

"What should we do about *this*?" he said, swinging his knife a few inches away from Clover's cock and balls.

"Should we remove her *unnatural* bits before we send her up in flames?"

"It will be more painful if we leave them *on* while she burns," the farmer said. "I want my daughter to see what happens to men who try to steal her virtue."

While two of the men grabbed Clover kicking and screaming out of the side of the barn, the rest of the mob carried a bunch of hay bales, piling them in a tall circle with a wooden pole placed in the center. As they pulled Clover toward the mound, she stared at the farmgirl with frightened eyes.

"Tell them I didn't rape you," she mumbled under her tight gag. "Tell them—"

"I'm sorry," the girl said with tears streaming down her face, afraid to tell her father the truth.

"Then get my friends, please!" Clover grunted, tilting her head in the direction of the apple orchard. "They can help me!"

The girl simply looked at Clover with a vacant expression, then stepped back toward the perimeter of the circle that had formed to watch the spectacle.

"Tara!" Clover screamed, flailing against her bonds. "Jessop!"

But the tight cloth binding her lips made it difficult for her to raise her voice barely above a whisper.

As the men lifted her onto the hay bales and began tying her hands behind the stake, she could hardly believe what was happening.

Please let this be a dream, Clover thought to herself, closing her eyes tightly. *This whole adventure has been so fantastical, it can't possibly be real.*

When she opened her eyes again looking for the girl,

hoping to find the one person who could still save her from her grisly fate, she'd already disappeared.

Clover was all alone, standing atop the makeshift platform, realizing her fantasy adventure was about to end in the worst possible way.

6

———

When Tara and Jessop saw the barn door closed, they assumed Clover wanted some more privacy, and they joked amongst themselves while they leisurely picked the apples, resting in the orchard enjoying an impromptu lunch.

Suddenly, the farmgirl rushed up to them panting and crying, looking at them with a terrified look in her face.

"Come quickly!" she said. "Your friend is in danger. My father found us in the barn and he's planning to burn her alive!"

"He's *what?*" Tara said, leaping to her feet.

"He thinks she's a witch! The whole town has assembled to watch the lynching. We've only got a few more minutes...!"

Tara looked up, noticing a thin plume of smoke rising over the top of the barn from the opposite side.

"I hope you've still got those special swordsman skills," she said, nodding toward Jessop. "Because we're going to need all the help we can get extricating ourselves from this predicament."

"How do you want to tackle this?" Jessop said as they all began running in the direction of the barn.

"How many people do you estimate have gathered?" Tara said, turning toward the girl.

"I don't know, maybe a hundred or so..."

"You circle around from the left," Tara nodded toward Jessop. "I'll try to keep them distracted from the other side while you free Clover. Then let's get the hell out of this place as quickly as we can!"

Tara and Jessop nodded at one another and as they circled around the barn from opposite directions, their eyes flew open in horror. Clover was standing atop the burning pile of hay while the flames moved closer to her body as she twisted and writhed against the pole, trying to free her hands.

Without hesitation, Tara suddenly began flinging arrows from her bow at lighting speed, dropping the onlookers assembled around the circle like bowling pins. When Clover saw her friends, she screamed for help, glaring at the approaching flames with wide eyes. Jessop leaped through the fire onto the hay bales, and in one swift motion tore through her binds with his sword. Then he lifted her in his arms and leapt back onto the ground, rolling in the grass to extinguish the flames tearing away at their clothes.

As the rest of the mob began to circle around them, Jessop deftly waved his sword, cutting them down one by one. When the ringleader found a hole and broke through the ranks, Clover reared back and kicked him as hard as she could in his balls. He yelped in pain grabbing his crotch, then his head suddenly jerked back when one of Clover's arrows caught him in the middle of his back.

"Come on!" Tara said, grabbing Clover's hand. "There's

too many of them. Maybe we can escape through the cornfield."

The friends peered toward a line of tall, thick stalks about fifty feet away, then they dashed into the thicket, slashing and stumbling their way through the dense cover until they came to the side of a wide, raging river. Seeing the tops of the corn plants rapidly rustling toward them, they peered at one another, shaking their heads.

"Looks like there's no other way out of here," Tara said, motioning toward the river.

"All for one," Jessop nodded.

"One for all," Clover said, grabbing her friends' hands and leaping into the tumbling current.

As they tried to clutch onto overhead branches and thick boulders lying in the middle of the tumult, the three friends gasped for air, trying to stay above the roiling water.

"Whatever you do, don't let go," Tara grunted. "If we get separated, there's no telling if we'll be able to find each other again."

As they held on for dear life, the current seemed to grow faster and more tumultuous, until they heard a familiar roar in the distance.

"Is that what I think it is?" Clover said, peering at Tara and Jessop with wide eyes.

"I'm afraid so," Tara said, lifting her head up to see the river ahead dropping off. "Brace yourselves, we have no idea how far a drop this is going to be–"

Suddenly, the trio were flung into the air, and they glanced below them, watching the plume falling over a hundred feet into a dark pool below. As they kicked their feet in terror, within seconds they plunged into the deep abyss, waving their arms wildly to return to the surface. When they popped their heads above the water one by one, they looked at one another and smiled.

"Everyone okay?" Tara said.

"Miraculously, I'm still in one piece," Jessop nodded.

"I think I might have *lost* a couple..." Clover said, reaching between her legs to feel her smooth vulva. "But everything *else* seems back to normal."

"Just in time," Tara sighed. "That weapon you chose from the mage has been more trouble than it was worth. I hope you've gotten your fill of enough pussy to keep you happy for a while."

"I can never have enough pussy," Clover grinned at Tara. "But from now on, I'll be happy to squirt only my *girly* juices."

R eady for more erotic chills and thrills? Order the next exciting volume in Clover's Fantasy Adventures:

Some sea creatures have certain evolutionary advantages...

ALSO BY VICTORIA RUSH

Wet your whistle a hundred different ways with Jade's Erotic Adventures. Browse the full collection of Victoria Rush steamy stories here:

Click to scan your favorites...

FOLLOW VICTORIA RUSH:

Want to keep informed of my latest erotic book releases? Sign up for my newsletter and receive a FREE bonus book:

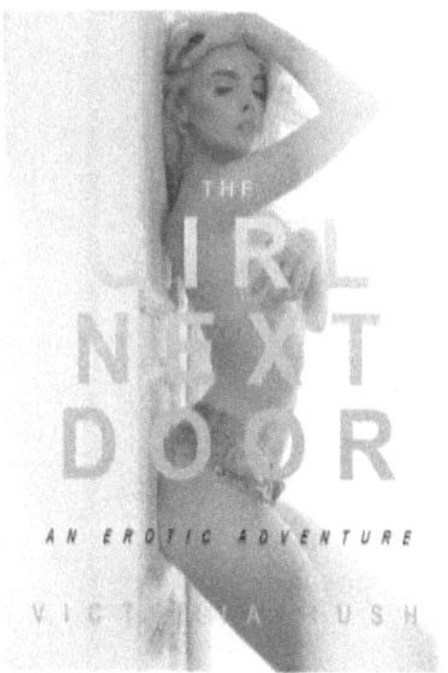

Spying on the neighbors just got a lot more interesting...